Who's Who at the Zoo?

By Ellen Weiss
Illustrated by Tom Cooke

A SESAME STREET/GOLDEN PRESS BOOK
Published by Western Publishing Company, Inc.
in conjunction with Children's Television Workshop.

©1987 Children's Television Workshop. Sesame Street puppet characters. ©Jim Henson Productions, Inc. 1987. All rights reserved. SESAME STREET and the SESAME STREET SIGN are registered trademarks and service marks of Children's Television Workshop. GOLDEN® and GOLDEN PRESS® are trademarks of Western Publishing Company, Inc. No part of this book may be reproduced or copied in any form without written permission from the publisher. Library of Congress Catalog Card Number: 87-82029 ISBN: 0-307-23157-7

Schmidt

It was a beautiful sunny day, and Big Bird, Ernie, and Bert went to the zoo. Big Bird was excited.

"I can't wait to see the ostrich! He's a big bird, too."

"I want to visit the pandas," said Ernie.

Bert said, "Look, there are some pigeons. Oh, happy day."

"Mr. Snuffleupagus asked me to say hello to his friend at the zoo. He asked me to give his friend these peanuts." Big Bird took a bag out of his backpack.

"Who is Snuffy's friend?" asked Ernie.

"Oh dear! I can't remember." Big Bird looked worried.

Then Bert said, "Do you mean that we're supposed to go see somebody, but we don't know who it is? How are we ever going to find Snuffy's friend, Big Bird?"

"Well, I do remember one thing Snuffy told me. His friend has four legs."

"That animal has four legs," said Ernie.
"That's a leopard," said Bert.
"Oh, hi, Mr. Leopard. But this is not Snuffy's friend. Snuffy's friend doesn't have spots," said Big Bird.

"Well, then, maybe it's that rhinoceros. She has four legs, and she doesn't have any spots," said Ernie.

But Big Bird shook his head. "No, I don't think so. I'm sure Snuffy would have told me if his friend had a great big horn like that."

"Look at those lions! Lions have four legs and no horns. One of them must be Snuffy's friend," said Ernie.

Big Bird sighed. "I don't think so. Snuffy didn't say anything about a mane, and those lions have big furry manes of hair."

Then Bert spotted something.
"Here are the pandas. Maybe that one is Snuffy's friend, Big Bird! He doesn't have a mane."
But Big Bird was not convinced. "I don't know. Look at those claws. I'm sure Snuffy's friend doesn't have claws."

"This chimpanzee doesn't have claws, Big Bird," said Ernie.
"That's true, but he has hands. Snuffy would have told me if his friend had real hands!"

"Oh, there's the zebra. Maybe she's Mr. Snuffleupagus' friend," said Ernie.
Big Bird thought about it. "No, I'm sure Snuffy would have said something about the zebra's black and white stripes. I don't think the zebra is Snuffy's friend."

"What about the giraffe? Maybe he's Snuffy's friend," said Ernie.
Big Bird replied, "I think Snuffy would have mentioned it if his friend had such a long neck."

"Oh, look, here's the ostrich! Hello Mr. Ostrich!" Big Bird cried.

But Bert looked doubtful. "I'm sure he's not Snuffy's friend. He only has two legs, and he has feathers!

"Now wait just a second Big Bird. All you've told us about Snuffy's friend is that he has four legs. What else do you know about him?"

"Well, let's see. Snuffy said his friend had wrinkly skin," said Big Bird.
"Maybe he's a giant tortoise like that one over there," said Ernie. "I'll bet he even has wrinkles under his shell."

"I don't think it's a tortoise. I just remembered that Snuffy's friend has big ears," said Big Bird.

Bert looked thoughtful. "Big ears? Maybe it's a rabbit!"

"No, it can't be a rabbit. Snuffy's friend is very big," said Big Bird.

Then Ernie shouted, "I know! The hippopotamus! He has four legs, wrinkly skin, and he certainly is big!"

"But the hippopotamus does not have a snuffle," said Big Bird.

Bert looked shocked. "A snuffle!? You didn't say anything about a snuffle! We'll never find an animal in the zoo with a snuffle!"

"Look! Mr. Elephant has a great big snuffle!" yelled Big Bird.
"That's a trunk," said Bert.
"It looks just like a snuffle to me. And he has four legs, wrinkly skin, huge ears, and he's very big," said Big Bird.
"Yes, but does he like peanuts?" asked Ernie.